ATTACK OF THE ROBOTS

ATTACK OF THE ROBOTS

BY GREG FARSHTEY

SCHOLASTIC INC.

New York   Toronto   London   Auckland   Sydney
Mexico City   New Delhi   Hong Kong   Buenos Aires

ISBN 0-439-82809-0

12 11 10 9 8 7 6 5 4 3 2   7 8 9 10 11/0

Printed in the U.S.A.
First printing, December 2006

Meca One, leader of the robot rebellion, stood on a catwalk overlooking an army of Devastator robots. Today was going to change the course of history on Sentai Mountain. Meca One was finally ready to reveal the secret battle machine that would bring the robots victory over the humans.

At one time, humans had ruled the entire mountain. To help them with mining and other dangerous tasks, the humans had built robots. But one day, the robot miners turned evil and rebelled against the humans. The energies unleashed during battle were so powerful that they split Sentai Mountain in half!

The humans won the first battle and

forced the robots down into the bottom of the gorge between the two halves of the mountain. With the robots gone, peace was restored and bridges were built to link the two sides of the mountain together again. But this victory was only temporary. The robots attacked again and took control of the southern half of the mountain.

Since then, the humans and robots had been locked in battle — mostly over control of the bridges. For whoever controlled the bridges would also control the mountain.

Now all that was about to end. With this new battle machine, the robot army would

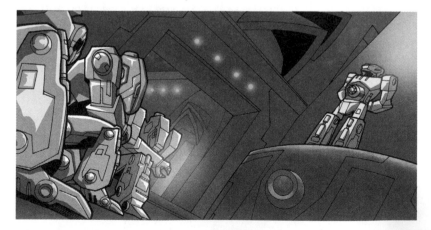

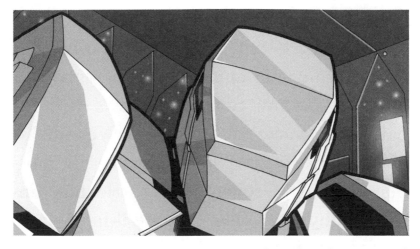

be able to storm across the bridges and attack Sentai Fortress itself. The fortress was home to the EXO-FORCE team — a special squad of human pilots who were responsible for keeping the human side of the mountain safe. That, too, would end today.

Meca One looked around. The robots had worked hard for this moment. All of the Devastator robot pilots were assembled and waiting for the news. It was time to show them the future of the robot army.

"Devastator units, prepare to receive

input," Meca One said. "Analysis: EXO-FORCE battle machines will be unable to defeat the battle machine you are about to see. Conclusion: Sentai Fortress will fall before the power of . . . Striking Venom!"

Suddenly, the lights in the chamber blazed on and revealed a battle machine unlike anything else. The Striking Venom was a huge, four-legged machine that resembled a green and black spider. Each leg was at least sixty feet high and featured a special claw that could grip on any terrain. Just above each claw was a battle post for an

armed Iron Drone robot. The battle post was both a place for the robot to ride securely and a mini power recharging station.

The true power of the Striking Venom was not in its size or even in the huge distances it could cover in a matter of seconds — it was in the center of the battle machine. The cockpit was armed with machine laser cannons and protected by two Iron Drones. The cockpit was empty at the moment. Each

Devastator calculated the odds that it would be chosen by Meca One to guide the armored giant into battle.

But Meca One had other plans. "This unit will pilot the Striking Venom," the gold robot announced. "Sentai Fortress will be ground to dust. Once we control both sides of the mountain, we will advance on the human settlements. We will bring logic, order, and robot rule to the humans. They will learn to obey the superior species."

There were no cheers or shouts of "Victory!" Unable to feel any emotion, the robots stood silently. But their processors were rapidly running through every possible outcome of the battle about to begin. All of the results were the same. . . .

The day of the humans was over. The day of the robots had arrived.

光　　光　　光

Hikaru flew the Silent Strike high above the EXO-FORCE test chamber. This was his sixth attempt at executing a very complex maneuver, and so far he had not been able to get it right.

Loop . . . roll . . . thrust . . . shoot, he repeated again

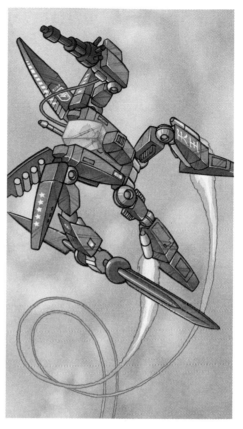

and again. In his old battle machine, the Stealth Hunter, this would have been easy. But the Silent Strike was faster and more powerful, and he was having trouble keeping it under control. Hikaru tried the loop one more time, but once again he ended up out of position to hit his target. He knew he had better master this battle machine quickly if he wanted to use it in a real fight.

Suddenly, Takeshi's voice blasted over his cockpit radio. "Hikaru! We need you on the ground!"

Hikaru looked below to see that his friend Takeshi was waving at him. He brought the Silent Strike to a landing and got out of the battle machine. "What's up, Takeshi? I was working on some new maneuvers."

"All training has been canceled, by order of Sensei Keiken," said Takeshi. "All EXO-FORCE pilots are to report for an emergency briefing immediately."

The two young men raced down the hallway to the central briefing chamber. The other pilots were already there. Sensei Keiken and Ryo, EXO-FORCE's best engineer, were standing on the platform.

"We have a great deal to discuss, so

let's not waste time," the Sensei said. "Ryo, please show us what you've found."

Ryo turned on the main viewscreen. It showed a chart of how much power the robots had been using in their fortress. The data came from special scanners mounted high up on the mountain. The bars on the chart were all about the same height, except for the last one, which was much higher.

"That's a power spike," Ryo said, pointing to the last bar. "We believe that the robots have constructed the biggest battle machine we've ever seen. Based on plans recovered during a recon mission, we have the blueprint for the robots' newest machine — the Striking Venom. "

The pilots looked at each other with concern. Sensei Keiken nodded at Ryo, who

changed the image on the screen to the machine's blueprint.

"Our engineers have studied the Striking Venom, hoping to determine just how strong it is and how we can stop it. I regret to say that so far we have not discovered a weakness."

Ryo shut off the screen. Keiken took a moment to collect himself before he continued speaking. "The Striking Venom is the greatest threat we have ever faced. I fear that if we cannot stop it, then the EXO-FORCE team and Sentai Fortress will be destroyed. The robots will be able to march on any settlement they wish. The future of humanity may depend on what we do today."

One of the pilots stood up. "I thought that the robots couldn't create any new battle machines . . . that all they could do was use the ideas of their human prisoners?"

"That's true," Keiken answered. "Whoever came up with the idea for Striking Venom must still be a prisoner on the other side of the mountain. Sadly, there is no time to stage a rescue. Ryo's scanners show the robots are on the march now — and we have to stop them before they reach this fortress."

Keiken looked out at the assembled pilots as if it might be the last time he would ever see them.

"Go to your battle machines. Prepare for the fight. It's time to power up!"

CHAPTER 2

The alarm was already sounding as Takeshi and Hikaru climbed into their battle machines — the Grand Titan and the Silent Strike. The Striking Venom had been seen making its way toward the bridges that spanned the gorge. An army of robot Sentries, R-1 Rammers, Thunder Furies, Sonic Phantoms, and Fire Vultures were ahead of it. Meca One was throwing its entire army into this attack.

"This is it," said Hikaru over the speaker. "Takeshi, if we don't come back, I want you to know —"

"We'll make it back," said Takeshi, smiling. "We have to. You still owe me a rematch after our last training battle, remember? You're not going to get out of it this easily."

The two friends emerged from the hangar, ready for battle. But they weren't the only ones. Engineers were scrambling to complete work on hastily built gates to reinforce Tenchii Bridge. The sky and ground were filled with human-piloted battle machines practicing fighting maneuvers. The communications channels were abuzz with pilots reporting the status of their weapons. Gunners manning laser cannons were stationed high up on the Sentai Fortress walls. Ha-Ya-To, in the Gate Guardian, was hovering about halfway across Tenchii Bridge, watching for trouble.

Just outside the hangar, Ryo was in his Uplink armor, doing a last-minute tune-up on the Mobile Defense Tank. Once that was done, he climbed out of Uplink and got behind the controls of the tank.

Takeshi looked far into the distance. Even though the Striking Venom was still a long way away, it seemed like it was right on top of him. Takeshi could also just make out the shape of hundreds of other robot battle machines charging in front of the Striking Venom. How could the EXO-FORCE survive in a fight against an army

that size and still have the strength to destroy the Striking Venom?

Unless we didn't attack the robot army from the front, he thought. *What if we could hit it from behind?*

Takeshi made a decision. If the Striking Venom could be beaten — even if it cost him his life — then the battle might be over before it started. He knew the other pilots would try to talk him out of his plan. Fortunately, they were all too busy to notice him slipping away.

Good-bye, Hikaru, he thought. *You risked your life to save my family from the robots. The least I can do is risk mine to save you and everyone else here.*

Takeshi thought fast. Not long ago, a robot strike team had surprised the humans by drilling up through the mountain and suddenly appearing in front of a bridge gate. Takeshi had helped the EXO-FORCE team drive the robots away and then seal the tun-

nel. Now he would use that tunnel to surprise the robots.

I hope they like surprises, he thought. *'Cause this one is going to be a whopper.*

Using his rotating laser cannon, he blasted away the debris covering the tunnel mouth. As Takeshi climbed down into the tunnel, he realized this might be his last journey into battle.

光　　光　　光

The fight was on! Advance lines of Sentries were probing the human defenses, making quick hit-and-run attacks on the gate in the center of Tenchii Bridge. The human guards drove them off each time, but it took precious laser energy to do so. If the laser cannon power cells ran out during the battle, nothing would keep the robots from getting through the gates.

Up in the sky, Hikaru and his squadron were fighting off Fire Vultures and Sonic Phantoms. The robots were not fighting with any great skill or using a complicated battle plan.

They are just trying to keep us busy, Hikaru realized. *They want to give Striking*

Venom time to get into position. And the worst thing is, their plan is working!

One of the cannons mounted above the Striking Venom cockpit fired a blast. It struck the ground near one of the bridges, carving out a thirty-foot-wide crater. Inside the Silent Strike, Hikaru shuddered. *How can we ever hope to defeat a monster machine like that?*

光 光 光

Deep underground, Takeshi had reached the end of the first half of the robot tunnel. He was now at the base of a small wooden bridge that connected the northern and southern halves of the mountain.

He crossed the bridge and descended into the second half of the tunnel. This part of the tunnel would lead him to the robot side of the mountain, but Takeshi did not plan to follow it the entire way. He checked his sensors but got only fuzzy readings because he was so deep underground. Despite the static, Takeshi managed to get an approximate location of the Striking Venom high above. If he tunneled up through the mountain at just the right spot, he would come out behind it.

He aimed his laser cannon and fired at the tunnel ceiling. Rock and dust rained down. *Going up,* he said to himself. *Next stop, giant robot spider.* He fired again and again, carving himself a new path to the surface. When he was far enough along, he made the Grand Titan's powerful pincers grab hold of the jagged rock wall and pull itself into the tunnel. As the Grand Titan scaled the rock wall, Takeshi checked his

sensors. The Striking Venom had stopped moving! This might be his only chance at stopping the Striking Venom. Takeshi quickened his pace toward the surface.

光　光　光

"Team, I'm going to need more time to study the Striking Venom if I'm gonna figure out a way to beat it!" Ryo's message blared over the other EXO-FORCE pilots' speakers. They got his message loud and clear. They were going to have to buy Ryo some time by preventing the robot army from advancing any farther across the bridge.

The well-trained team burst into action. Stealth Hunters used their laser rifles to bring down trees and create rock-slides along the robots' path. As Ryo advanced closer to the Striking Venom to get a better look, his Mobile Defense Tank

blasted dozens of Sentries to clear a path for his vehicle.

Meca One had not expected EXO-FORCE to take this sort of action. The robot's processors jumped into action. *Conclusion: If the EXO-FORCE is on the offensive, then they must have found a way to counter the Striking Venom.*

Ryo smiled when he saw the Striking Venom stop advancing. *Good work, team,* Ryo thought. *This buys me some time.*

Ryo and his copilot drove the Mobile Defense Tank forward to get a better look at the Striking Venom. It was dangerous, but this was the only way to find the Striking Venom's weakness. The tank blasted a path through the robot battle machines on the bridge. As quickly as the path was opened, more robots advanced forward and closed it up. By the time Ryo got the tank close to the Striking Venom, the path behind, back to Sentai Fortress, was blocked by robot rubble.

The Striking Venom looked even tougher than it had in the blueprints. He guessed the armor on the huge battle machine was at least a foot thick, if not more. The laser cannons mounted on top were more powerful than anything the robots had ever made before. Compared to Striking Venom, the human battle machines were toys.

Ryo aimed and fired all his weapons at the gigantic robot battle machine. *If this is going to be EXO-FORCE's last battle,* he said to himself, *at least we'll go down fighting.*

The blasts bounced off the Striking Venom's armor. One of the Striking Venom's machine laser cannons took aim at the Mobile Defense Tank and fired, shattering the ground in front of the tank. The next blast sent the tank tumbling end over end. Ryo and his co-pilot scrambled out and took cover.

Two shots, Ryo thought. *It only took the Striking Venom two shots to badly damage the tank. It's going to take a miracle to win this battle.*

CHAPTER 3

Meca One checked its scanners. The battle was back on track. The EXO-FORCE pilots were starting to retreat, although they were fighting every inch of the way. It was time for Striking Venom to cross the Tenchii Bridge and end this battle once and for all. He hit the controls and started the battle machine moving forward again.

Suddenly, alarms blared inside the cockpit. Scanners showed an enemy battle machine — the Grand Titan — attacking from behind!

Meca One slammed a red button that would lock all weapons systems on to the new attacker. Then it opened a communications channel to the Iron Drones that were stationed on the legs and body of the Striking Venom.

"Open fire on the Grand Titan," Meca One ordered. "It must be stopped!"

The Grand Titan had emerged from the tunnel only a few feet behind the Striking Venom. As Takeshi had hoped, there were no other robot battle machines nearby. It was just him and the robots' ultimate weapon.

Here we go, Takeshi thought. *Maybe this will teach the robots not to come over without an invitation.*

He fired Grand Titan's laser cannon several times, aiming at the joints where the spiderlike legs attached to the body. The blasts were on target, but the joints were almost as heavily armored as the rest of the battle machine. The Grand Titan managed only to make a few dents and scratches to the Striking Venom — not nearly enough to stop the monstrous battle machine.

Okay, time for Plan B, Takeshi thought. *Too bad I don't have a Plan B.*

The Iron Drones stationed on the legs opened fire with their hand lasers. Takeshi fired back, forcing them to abandon their positions and take cover. But Takeshi's victory was only temporary — the Striking Venom was taking aim at him now. The first blast missed, but the shock wave from it still managed to knock the Grand Titan off its feet.

Before the Striking Venom could fire a second time, a blast hit it from the front. Takeshi saw it was Ryo standing on top of the battered Mobile Defense Tank, aiming and firing the vehicle's weapon by hand. *Let's make things interesting,* Takeshi thought, *firing his own laser cannon at the Striking Venom.*

"Takeshi, my copilot and I have to get out of here!" Ryo radioed. "The tank is a mess and the laser cannon's power cells are empty. Come back with us!"

"You go ahead," Takeshi answered. "I'm not done here yet."

Ryo agreed, though Takeshi could tell he wasn't happy about it. He and his copilot climbed down into the tunnel Takeshi had made. With luck, they would make it back safely to the fortress.

When the robot battle machine's right front leg lifted to take a step closer to the Tenchii Bridge, Takeshi suddenly had an idea. He blasted the ground right where the spider's leg would come down. When the Striking Venom stepped forward into the crater left by Takeshi's blast, the robot battle machine was thrown off balance.

"Grand Titan, one. Striking Venom, zero!" Takeshi shouted. "Next time, watch your step, you bucket of bolts!"

Takeshi took this chance to charge forward. He grabbed one of the Striking Venom's legs with his battle machine's electromagnetic pulse pincer. The pincer was designed to send a jolt of energy through an enemy machine that would temporarily shut down all systems. If it worked, the Striking Venom would be just another hunk of junk.

Just as Takeshi released the pulse, alarms went off in the Grand Titan's cockpit. Something was wrong! The Striking Venom had managed to deflect the pulse. Now the Grand Titan was being blasted by its own electromagnetic pulse!

Instantly, the Grand Titan's scanners went black and all weapons systems turned off. *Oh, no!* thought Takeshi. *The Grand Titan won't be able to reboot for fifteen minutes. Somehow, I don't think the Striking Venom will give me a time-out!*

光　光　光

Up in the sky, not far from the EXO-FORCE fortress, Hikaru was fighting for his life.

The EXO-FORCE team's tactics had managed to slow the robots down temporarily, but that was over now. If a robot battle machine got damaged, the ones behind it would just push it out of the way and keep going. Robot engineers blasted away piles of rock and rubble so the army could continue to move.

In all the months he had been an EXO-FORCE pilot, he had never seen so many battle machines on the attack. For every

Fire Vulture he knocked out of the sky, it seemed like six more took its place. He had fired his laser rifle so many times that he was afraid the barrel might melt. And still the enemy kept coming, determined to destroy Sentai Fortress.

A flash of red caught Hikaru's eye. Something was streaking through the air like a rocket toward the fortress. The Silent Strike's scanners started buzzing, indicating they had identified the flying object. It was the Grand Titan!

Wait a minute, thought Hikaru. *The Grand Titan can't fly!*

He triggered the Silent Strike's boot

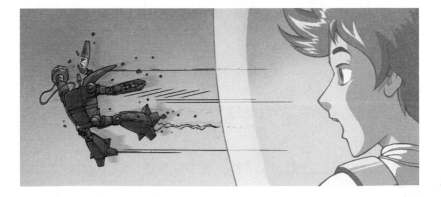

jets and zoomed off in pursuit. As he got closer, he could see the Grand Titan wasn't actually flying. It was tumbling end over end through the sky, as if something had thrown it at high speed . . . and the only battle machine strong enough to do that was the Striking Venom. If Hikaru didn't catch the Grand Titan, it would smash right into the EXO-FORCE fortress.

Nobody's using the Grand Titan as a bowling ball while I'm around, Hikaru thought. *I'm going to catch it, even if it means I crash, too.*

The Silent Strike flew after the Grand Titan at top speed. It was flying so fast, Hikaru could barely keep the battle machine under control. But he was getting closer every second.

Come on, come on, Hikaru thought to himself. *Just a little closer . . . I've almost got it!*

The hands of the Silent Strike grabbed

on to the arm of the Grand Titan. Warning alarms went off all through Hikaru's battle machine. The momentum of the Grand Titan threatened to pull the Silent Strike apart. Hikaru activated his battle machine's retro-rockets, which worked like brakes. Little by little, the two battle machines began to slow down.

Down below, Ryo and his copilot were just emerging from the tunnel when they caught sight of what was going on. Ryo sped off for the fortress to get his Uplink armor. *Takeshi and Hikaru will need my help,* he thought. *If there's anything left of either of them, that is!*

Hikaru brought the Silent Strike in for a safe, if rough, landing, with the Grand Titan in its grip. The Grand Titan was battered, dented, and cracked — and Takeshi didn't look so good, either. Hikaru brought the Grand Titan inside the hangar and found Ryo waiting to make repairs.

"This'll take weeks to fix!" Ryo said as he scanned the damage.

Takeshi's eyes flickered open. "You don't have . . . weeks, . . . Ryo. You have minutes."

"Are you all right?" asked Hikaru, helping Takeshi out of the Grand Titan. "What happened out there?"

"I tried to beat the Striking Venom on

my own," Takeshi answered. "But it tossed me aside like trash."

"You're crazy!" Hikaru snapped. "You could have been killed! And for what? No single battle machine is going to be able to beat the Striking Venom!"

Takeshi smiled knowingly. "You're wrong, Hikaru. Yeah, I got pounded and my battle machine is a mess. But it was worth it."

"How?" asked Hikaru.

"Now I know how to beat the Striking Venom," answered Takeshi. "And we're going to do it together."

CHAPTER 4

"Pull back! Pull back!" Ha-Ya-To yelled into his cockpit microphone. From his location directly in front of Sentai Fortress, he could see that the EXO-FORCE team was losing the battle. Sentries had broken through the gates on Tenchii Bridge and were advancing on the fortress. Human pilots had been forced to abandon their damaged battle machines. Worse, the Striking Venom was starting to cross the bridge as well.

The EXO-FORCE battle machines began a fighting retreat toward the fortress. Outnumbered and overpowered, the best they were able to do was delay the attacking robots.

Maybe the humans can make a stand

somewhere else, Ha-Ya-To thought. *All we can do now is hope.*

"Form a line on our side of Tenchii Bridge!" Ha-Ya-To shouted into his cockpit microphone. "Aim for the arms and legs of the battle machines, where the armor is thinnest! Fire all lasers!"

光　　光　　光

Sensei Keiken watched the battle from inside the fortress. He had never been more afraid for the future of humanity. At the same time, he had never been more proud of the members of the EXO-FORCE team. They had started out as young, inexperienced pilots with no idea how to work together. Now they were fighting like veterans and showing the robots how brave humans could be.

"Sensei, you must leave," said his aide. "The robots will reach the fortress in a matter of minutes! You must not be captured!"

"Where are Takeshi, Hikaru, and Ryo?" the Sensei asked.

"In the main hangar. The Grand Titan was badly damaged and Ryo is trying desper-

ately to repair it."

The Sensei nodded. "Regardless of how this battle plays out, we have learned something."

"What is that, Sensei?"

"We cannot beat

the robots by using the same power and the same weapons as they have. They will always be able to build more battle machines — and build them faster than we can. If we are going to try to just outfight them, we will lose. We have to outsmart them."

"How?" asked the aide, looking confused.

"We have to find a new kind of power . . . something the robots cannot master. There is a place I heard of, many years ago — a place some think is a myth. But if it is real, we must find it. It may be the key to defeating the robot army."

Sensei Keiken turned and headed for the main hangar. "And we will look for it . . . if we manage to survive this battle."

光　光　光

Hikaru took a deep breath and leaned against the hangar wall. It was all clear to him now. His friend Takeshi had lost his mind.

"You're going to go back out there, against the Striking Venom, in armor that is being held together with wire and hope?" Hikaru asked. "And you're — excuse me, *we're* — going to beat that six-story-high pile of nuts and bolts?"

"That's right," Takeshi answered with a smile.

Hikaru turned to Ryo. "Tell me he got hit on the head."

"It wouldn't matter," Ryo chuckled. "His skull's so thick, he would never notice."

Takeshi leaned over Ryo's shoulder as he worked. "You need to wire the laser cannon this way. If you do it that way —"

"You'll live through the battle?" Ryo finished his sentence, with more than a little disbelief. "If I do it the way you suggested, you'll wind up a pile of ash."

"What's going on here?" demanded the Sensei, rushing into the hangar. "The battle is out there, not in here!"

"Please, Sensei!" said Takeshi. "I have an idea. I think we can win!" Before Keiken could object, Takeshi continued. "The Striking Venom fried the Grand Titan by deflecting my electromagnetic pulse. That's why I lost. Then I realized — maybe draining all the power out of one of our battle machines is the one way to beat that metal monster."

A nearby blast sent a tremor through the fortress.

"The Striking Venom has one vulnerable spot — directly underneath the cockpit," Takeshi said quickly. "The armor is not any thinner there, but that's the one place that the cannons can't aim at you. The only thing you'd have to worry about is hand laser fire coming from the Iron Drones on the legs."

"Then what?" said the Sensei. "You won't have more than a few seconds underneath the cockpit before the Striking Venom moves."

"One shot with the laser cannon," Takeshi said. "There would be just time for that. If I channel every bit of power in the Grand Titan — all the weapon power, the movement energy, every last bit — into that one blast, we might have a chance. It will leave my battle machine dead, but if it works . . ."

"It's crazy," said Hikaru. "You'll get killed."

"No," said the Sensei. "It might just work."

"Then let me do it in the Stealth Hunter," said Hikaru. "That armor is intact. The Grand Titan is falling apart."

"The Stealth Hunter isn't powerful enough," said Takeshi.

The Sensei made a quick decision and said, "Ryo, finish your repairs on the Grand Titan. Bring in a team to help you if you have to, and when you're done, get to work on the Stealth Hunter. I want it in the air!"

BA-WHOOM!

The fortress shook from a blast by the Striking Venom. Dust and small bits of rock fell from the hangar ceiling. They could

hear the shouts of EXO-FORCE pilots and the whine of laser fire.

"And you better do it fast," the Sensei finished.

CHAPTER 5

By the time Hikaru flew the powered-up Stealth Hunter out of the fortress, the situation had gone from bad to worse. The EXO-FORCE defenders had been driven back to the fortress walls. Pilots crouched behind the smoking hulks of their battle machines and now fought only with hand lasers. The Striking Venom had crossed the Tenchii Bridge and was firing at will, trying to breach the main gate of the fortress.

From the air, Hikaru spotted Meca One in the cockpit of the massive battle machine. This was the robot that had caused so much pain and destruction. Hikaru was tempted to send the Stealth Hunter into a dive and take out the gold robot on his own.

But he had promised the Sensei and Takeshi that he would stick to the plan.

"Hey, chrome dome!" he yelled through the Stealth Hunter's speakers. "Nice metal bug you got there! Too bad I left my swatter in my other battle machine."

Meca One glanced up at the Stealth Hunter. The Striking Venom reared back so that its machine laser cannons pointed upward. Both cannons fired. Just as planned, Hikaru dodged the attack.

"Some army you've got!" Hikaru laughed. "I could beat the whole lot of you with a can opener!"

The Stealth Hunter's sensor screen flashed. Half a dozen Fire Vultures were closing in fast. Hikaru beamed a signal to Ha-Ya-To in the Gate Guardian battle machine. Ha-Ya-To immediately broke off the fight he was in and led a squadron of flyers against the Fire Vultures, leaving Hikaru free to concentrate on the Striking Venom.

Meca One continued firing on the Stealth Hunter, even though it knew the humans had tracking computers that helped them dodge blasts. But while the humans were evading one weapon, they were great targets for another. Meca One's metal finger hit a button that triggered the launch of an energy disc. The disc flew in a wide arc and came at the Stealth Hunter from the side.

Hikaru noticed the incoming object too late. It hit his battle machine and magnetized itself to the armor. Meca One was trying to fry the Stealth Hunter! Energy poured from the disc into the Stealth Hunter's circuitry. Hikaru could smell wiring starting to melt.

Just what I need, Hikaru said to himself. *Baked battle machine.*

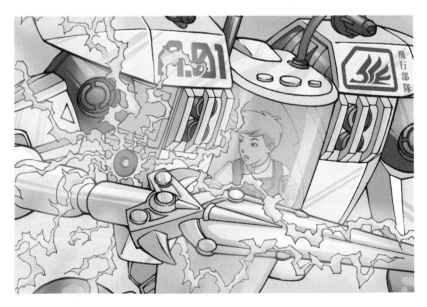

He glanced at the ground. The Grand Titan was making its way toward the Striking Venom, with other EXO-FORCE battle machines providing cover. Meca One had to be distracted for at least another minute. That meant the Stealth Hunter had to stay in the air.

Desperate, Hikaru powered up the Stealth Hunter's electro-sword. He swung the sword at the disc in an attempt to cut it free. The effort succeeded, but at a cost. The disc came loose, but took a portion of the Stealth Hunter's armor with it. One lucky shot by a robot at the now exposed circuits, and the Stealth Hunter would go down in flames.

"Nice try!" Hikaru broadcasted to Meca One. "Now you owe me a new battle machine! Maybe I'll make one out of spider scrap!"

Down below, just as they had planned, Takeshi had managed to maneuver the Grand Titan underneath the Striking Venom. As other EXO-FORCE pilots blasted away at any battle machines that came too near, Takeshi aimed the Grand Titan's laser cannon straight up at the underside of the Striking Venom's cockpit.

Takeshi hit the button on the controls that would begin channeling all the battle machine's power into the laser. It took only a fraction of a second to do its work. The Grand Titan now had no communications, no ability to move, and no way to use any weapon besides the laser cannon. Takeshi would get one shot at the Striking Venom, and after that, it would be completely powerless.

Seeing that Takeshi was ready, the Stealth Hunter swooped down from the sky, firing its ultra-powered laser rifle. The Striking Venom fired back, all of its weapons trained on the flying battle machine. Just as they had planned, the Striking Venom was too busy with the Stealth Hunter to notice the Grand Titan.

"Here we go," Takeshi said to himself

as he triggered the laser cannon. There was a loud hum, a bright flash — and then nothing. It hadn't worked!

"Great! Just great!" Takeshi yelled. "I can't even get my own battle machine to go dead when I want it to!"

Takeshi tore open the control console to see what was wrong. One of the wiring jobs Ryo had done had come loose. Takeshi scrambled to reconnect it as the Striking Venom drove the Stealth Hunter back with the power of its laser cannons.

It was done! Takeshi crossed his fingers and fired the laser cannon again.

A bolt of pure energy, more powerful than anything ever seen in the robot–human conflict, shot from the Grand Titan's laser cannon. It hit its mark dead-on! The blast pierced the Striking Venom's cockpit armor, shattering circuits and burning out controls. The Striking Venom lurched and almost fell

over. Two Iron Drones stationed near the cockpit tumbled off and hit the ground.

"Wahoo!" shouted Takeshi. He had completely disabled one of the Striking Venom's machine laser cannons. The second was smoking and helplessly turning from side to side.

In the cockpit, Meca One scanned the damage. Weapons systems were 96 percent damaged. The armor was pierced. Sensors were offline, and so was the targeting computer and all communications. The only thing that still worked was the power core, which allowed the Striking Venom to move.

The golden robot looked up at Sentai Fortress, so close to collapse, and saw something remarkable. The EXO-FORCE team, battered and beaten and on the verge of total defeat, was suddenly rallying. Pilots were climbing into barely functioning battle machines and charging at the robot attackers. Gunners on the fortress walls were clearing away the rubble around their weapons and firing again. The humans had caught a second wind and were forcing the robot battle machines to retreat!

It was only logical, Meca One concluded. The Striking Venom could not continue to fight until it received major repairs. Remaining on this side of the bridge would mean destruction. Meca One could not feel regret or anger. Its only concern was that the humans had found a weakness in the Striking Venom. Meca One had to return to the southern side of the mountain to fix this problem immediately. *Then Sentai Fortress will fall,* Meca One thought.

The Striking Venom took a giant step backward, almost smashing the Grand Titan into pieces. The Stealth Hunter flew down after it, firing its laser rifle, eager for a little revenge. Hikaru was going to pursue the Striking Venom, when the Sensei's voice crackled over the speakers.

"Let it go, Hikaru," he said. "Get Takeshi to safety. And . . . good work."

光　　光　　光

The battle was over.

The Striking Venom's retreat had been the signal for the rest of the robot army to follow. The robots had been so confident in the Striking Venom's power that they had not even considered what to do if it were defeated.

Every EXO-FORCE pilot knew how close they had come to defeat. They hurried to put up temporary gates and fix battle machines and wall cannons. Fortunately, all of the EXO-FORCE team members survived — some just barely — but many pilots would be without battle machines for a while.

The fortress was in bad shape as well. It would take many months, maybe even a year, to fully repair it. And even then, as the Sensei pointed out, the Striking Venom would just return and the battle would start again. The EXO-FORCE team needed to find a way to defeat the robots, totally and completely, and they needed to find it soon.

光　　光　　光

The Sensei summoned Ryo, Ha-Ya-To, Takeshi, and Hikaru to his chambers. "I want to thank all four of you for your bravery and your skill," the EXO-FORCE leader began. "Without you, we would not be here today."

The four pilots smiled, but said nothing. They knew it was the Sensei's time to speak.

"We have much to celebrate tonight," he continued. "But in another week, or month, or year, the robots will return, possibly with even greater weapons. We must be prepared to meet them and defeat them. That is why I have called you here. You are about to undertake your most important mission ever."

The Sensei looked at each pilot. They

were all courageous and completely dedicated to defeating the robots.

"The time has come for EXO-FORCE to power up in a way it never has before," Sensei Keiken said. "The time has come to find . . . the golden city."

Long into the night, the Sensei told his brave pilots of a legendary place of power. Dawn would bring the start of a new era for the EXO-FORCE team, one filled with greater dangers and the chance of even more amazing adventures.

The battle for Sentai Mountain had been won, for now . . . but the fight was far from over.

COMING SOON!

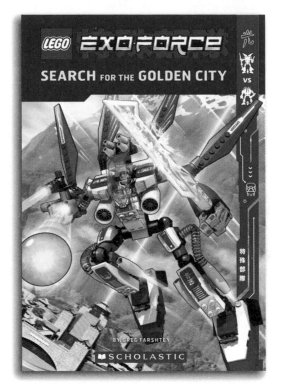

The last battle between the robots and the humans has left the **EXO-FORCE** fortress in ruins. Sensei Keiken believes that the humans have one remaining hope—the Golden City—a legendary place of power. Even if it does exist, can the **EXO-FORCE** team find it in time to save the humans?